MW01229497

Dark Peter
Christmas in Hell

By BW Bloodlust

Cover Art by Gregg Grant

Illustrated by Jadrienne Atkins

Foreword

Dear Readers,

The author of this book is a dear friend of mine. He has dreamed of writing a book and becoming an author his whole life. I am so proud to have had the ability to watch his dream grow. He loves horror and we love Christmas together. His favorite Christmas movie is Elf which shows his optimistic side. As an author and a reader, he enjoys anything by Clive Barker and Ramsay Campbell. As a child, he hid behind his dad's recliner and watched 1977's Snow Beast.

I have enjoyed watching him develop this character and his journey through the multitude of Christmas characters to destroy. His character development and his ability to bring them to life is just so beautiful. He did research on many of the characters of Christmas lore. Together, I helped him consider what characters were meant to be in the story. He found many more than he included in this story, but he thought these would be the most interesting to work with.

As an author, I was very inspired by his first non-short story. There is no way you won't enjoy his words.

Love,

JK Cobra

Prologue

Lapland Rovaniemi, Finland – The Arctic Circle. So cold, merely glacial, truly inhospitable. The endless winter of the unfriendly, unwelcoming tundra outside. Home of the indigenous people who worship the mother lights and the white war god. Also, the home of Saint Nicholas, sitting so high above the icy mountains overlooking the horizon where the sun refuses to rise for months at a time. The darkness hosting one of the most hellish environments and beings the world has ever known.

Santa
Claus

Chapter 1

The Awakening

Looking out of an icy, glazed window from a house on the frozen peaks; a chubby, white-bearded man dressed in brown furry overalls rounded spectacles back up onto the bridge of his nose. He gazes upon the frigid landscape, the icy winds that howl like a wild wolf seeking a pack. Beyond the frosty hostile terra firma, he can see a great evil festering – beginning its march against him, against everything that he has fought for; against humanity, itself. He slams his fist against the window sill, splinters riddling his hand as blood drizzles to the old, hardwood floor.

"Are you hurt, Sir Klaas?" One brave elf speaks out as the others watch the large figure in terror.

"I'm fine," he watches his blood drip like a faucet from his hand. "We're all in grave danger, lads." Looking at the gathered elves gathered around him. Looks of despair and fear fill their eyes. "Evil is coming. It may already be here."

Another no name elf speaks up, "You can defeat it, Sir Klaas! We believe in you!" Rallying the troop morale, they all start to cheer.

"No!" Waving his hand out, as a few droplets of blood strike the closest elves in their faces, making them tremble as they wipe it off on the wrapping paper and wreaths on the desk. "It's not that simple anymore! It has gotten to be more than I can handle," he lowers his head, "We NEED help."

The elves talk amongst themselves in a clattering of gibberish. "Who or what can we do to help you, Sir Klaas?" One of the elves speaks in a concerning voice.

"We have to fight this evil…with evil!" St. Nicholas points to a chain-locked door in the back of the room.

"The dark one, Sir Klaas?" One of the elves is appalled by the words spoken just moments before.

"Yes," he nods, placing his hand into the fuzzy pocket of his overalls and revealing an old skeleton key. "Bring him to me."

The elves, hesitantly, take the key from him and, reluctantly, comply with St. Nicholas's bidding. Once the chains are unlocked, they diligently travel down the tall spiral, stone stairwell – deep into the bowels of the icy mountains. They obey their master while daring not to speak the name of the one who lies below. Finally, they reach the bone-chilling crypt of their destination. The elves wave torches around a figure – one encased in a block of ice.

Alone and forgotten – frozen ages and ages ago – the elves begin the grueling task of melting the tiny iceberg. The defrosting process takes what seems endless – hours. Each droplet, sliding away from the ice and pitter-pattering against the floor, revealing more and more of the resident from the ice block.

The ice, finally, subsides as a figure of a dark-skinned male emerges – both tall and formidable. His face hosts a primitive facial expression trapped within his weather-worn profile. A thick, brawny chest, powerful arms, and tree trunk-like legs break free from the thawing ice prison.

One of the elves checks the figure's breathing by listening to his chest. He nods to his brothers as they work in unison to carry the herculean figure up the spiral, stone stairwell – grunting and whining from the weight the whole way. Finally, their task was accomplished – they completed St. Nicholas's bidding. They have delivered the hulking dark figure to their master. They cover him up in a woolen blanket as he still slumbers, dreaming of his endless icy cocoon.

The wreath-trimmed fireplace crackles and a set of charcoal eyes begin to blink briefly, then open completely to survey his surroundings.

St. Nicholas turns to see him, "Good to see you awake, brother," he says as he adjusts his glasses again upon his nose.

Elves

Chapter 2

Ice Melts

The man before St. Nicholas opens his mouth to speak, but cannot as words will not form from his lips, he begins to cough from the strain.

"Give him some water. He has been down there a very long time," he commands his elves to fetch a drink for his brother. They do so, the brother drinks in the cold arctic water, fulfilling his thirst. "Thirsty, eh?" He touches his nose again.

Breathing heavily, "Good to see you, too, brother, Sir Klaas, Saint Nicholas…Santa Claus. What are you calling yourself these days?" He tries to provoke St. Nicholas, scowling at him.

Crossing his arms, "All this time, brother. I thought you would have done some good…for once in your life," he says, extending his hand out to his brother.

He waves off St. Nicholas's hand, "Do not try to help me up now, brother; you've had me in your basement for… how long has it been?" He snarls at his brother.

"Eight hundred years? Give or take a couple of hundred?" He thinks over the question.

The elves all cower and try to hide as the massive figure stands upright, stretching his back and arms. "Eight… HUNDRED…years?" He raises his voice. "I never imagined you would be so cruel, brother."

"Nor I you, brother, or shall I call you Black Zwarte? Zwarte Piet?" His belly jiggles slightly with mirth.

"No, no, these names are dead to me. Just as you, for locking me up in that ice pit…forgetting about me."

"Not forgotten, just let's say put away a little while for your protection and everyone else's as well," he says while touching his nose again.

"Then, pray tell, brother? Tell me this? Why did you finally let me out of your freezer downstairs?" Cracking his knuckles. "Felt sorry for me? I'm going to punish you, brother! So sweareth Dark Peter!"

"Then, so be it!" St. Nicholas opens his arms to his brother. "Kill me, if you wish, brother…it's all going to be over soon…for all of us…anyway."

Dark Peter tilts his head, looking over St. Nicholas, intensely, "What, in the devil, are you talking about, brother? Have you gone senile in these many years?"

"No, brother. It is coming for all of us," he looks into Dark Peter's eyes deeply, "YOU included." He carries on the conversation after a brief pause, "They are all converging, working in unison, for a single purpose…not quite sure of that purpose, but I do know their desired result."

"Who? Who has threatened you, brother? Who has threatened the almighty Santa Claus?" He chastises Saint Nicholas.

Chapter 3

Hope

Staring straight into Dark Peter's onyx eyes, "All of them—every last one."

"And why, dear brother, would I care at all if they take you out? Tell me that," he declares his point, standing his ground.

"Don't fool yourself. Do you think for a split second that they will let you live? Ho, ho, ho! I think not, brother!" He expresses his views, "Once they are done with me, it will be your turn; the last of my lineage. Then, mankind will really suffer."

"You think for an instant that I give a damn about you? About mankind? Ha!" He scoffs at St. Nicholas.

Saint Nicholas grabs ahold of Dark Peter–one hand on each of his shoulders, "You don't get it! You never have, you damn fool," shaking him sharply.

Dark Peter's hand shoots out, backhanding his brother to the cold floor, "Do not touch me! If you think that there is no hope left, why do you care?"

Wiping the blood from his lip as he stands back up, "Because you are now the only hope…brother."

"Hmmmph! Can't make me a saint nor a savior." Dark Peter punches the heavy wooden door to the sturdy-built cabin. Splinters fly and the elves begin to scurry about like tiny cockroaches.

"No…you never wanted to be…but you can be one, brother. By my side," he touches his nose again.

"Maybe? Maybe I like being bad? Maybe I like being locked up in your freezer?" He cackles at St. Nicholas.

"There won't be a cold box to go back to, you can't see the urgency here. You never have. This was a mistake. How could I ever think you would be a savior for everyone…including yourself!" St. Nicholas points at Dark Peter.

"What do you want me to do?" Slamming his fists down over and over onto the stony fireplace. "I am not you. I am not good like you."

"Then be bad…be so bad that even you can't handle it. Be so damn good at being bad…" St. Nicholas begins to truly grin at his brother, Dark Peter.

Dark Peter's sinister grin joins his brother's, "THAT…I can do!"

"Come, brother; we shall discuss matters over broth and elk meat." St. Nicholas leads his brother into a room with a solid oak square table. The two sit down and start to talk through St. Nicholas's plan of action.

"I am not a patient man, Nicholas," he tears off a piece of meat with his teeth. "Where do I start?"

"A familiar foe…maybe a friend? Belsnickel?" St. Nicholas continues to try to explain the tasks at hand to his primal brother.

"Ah, an old ally from my past," he nods, "He will fall rather easily." Dark Peter stands from the table, anxious and excited to begin his work.

"Remember, brother, be weary of him for he serves a greater purpose now, more evil than ever before."

Dark Peter grimaces at St. Nicholas, "I am the biggest evil around. You would do well to remember that!" He takes leave of the house high in the mountains to begin his quest.

St. Nicholas walks to the door to yell to him as he leaves, "Seek out the evil, brother.

It will draw you to it." He watches Dark Peter vanish from his sight.

"I fear, Sir Klaas, he is barbaric and untamed…he is too destructive," one of the braver elves speaks up.

Without hesitation, "That is exactly what I am hoping for," he exhales deeply.

Artikos
the Polar Bear
God

Chapter 4

The Bear God

Santa Claus sits on his sofa chair, staring into the warm fireplace while sipping hot cider with two of his elves, "Sir Klaas, why was it so easy to get him to do your bidding?" One of the elves asks.

"Ho, ho, ho! It wasn't easy!" He chuckles sarcastically while pointing to his lip and face – showing off his Christmas bruises of multiple colors. "I tried to get him to see the light and do the right thing, but when I mentioned being bad…he was all for it."

"But…buy isn't that bad, sir?" The elves are frightened by Santa's answer.

"It is bad, but it was our only choice, to use his own anger and evil to goad him on."

The other elf who has been silent the entire time, takes a sip of cider, "I wonder where and what he's doing now?"

Sighing, Santa Claus answers, "Destroying something, wreaking havoc, it's all he has ever known." He gets up to look out of the window and sees a massive blizzard, beating down on the horizon.

Dark Peter treads through the storm as it pelts him with numbing winds and snow flakes – hard as rocks through his ragged shirt. The cold doesn't bother him, it's been his home for so long. His vision is limited, but he knows his path and it goes straight through the indigenous Sami's tribal people.

Primitive people of the arctic, indeed cut off from the rest of civilization – they know the legend of the intruder that now passes through their village and do not appreciate his presence at all. His large footsteps sound, interrupting the sound of carols being sung. Their decorations jostle about, falling to the ground.

Words and spears begin to fly about Dark Peter, both causing no harm to him, "Leave me be, peasants. My quarrel does not rest with you!" Swatting spears away with his bare hands. "Begone gnats! Waving his arms about trying to scare the natives away.

A rumbling sound shakes and vibrates the very ground and echoes muting out the howling winds.

"Thunder?" Dark Peter stops in his tracks as something emerges through the blinding snow, he places a hand above his eyes to get a clear look at what is making the rumbling noise in the distance. A mountain of snow moves. No, it's a mound of snow white fur coming into view.

"Artikos! Artikos!" One of the Sami shouts out, pointing at a towering polar bear.

"Ahhh, shit!" Dark Peter is no small man, but he is dwarfed by the Sami's Bear God. Standing over fifteen feet tall, his claws shine above everyone like crystals on an iced Christmas tree.

The remaining Sami tribesmen clap in applause of the gargantuan bear as it drops its massive weight and paws, the size of wagon wheels, down onto Dark Peter – crushing him to the ground.

Dark Peter screams out, but is held silent by being smothered by the giant bear. He punches and bites to try to get any sort of leverage – to escape the white mass of fur and muscles.

It rears back, suddenly, releasing Dark Peter from the prison that its body was creating. Six-inch claws take a swipe at Dark Peter, slashing his defined, rippling chest. Blood splatters through the windy air, marking the pristine white snow and decorated trees with crimson.

"Agggh! Damn you!" Dark Peter grabs his chest just as the great polar bear once again prepares to slam down upon him, "Not this time, Teddy." Dark Peter catches one of the massive paws and snaps off one of his razor claws.

"Aroooooo!" The bear howls, from immense pain and hunger, at Dark Peter. Jaws the size of prehistoric beasts clamp down upon Dark Peter's shoulder.

"Urrrnnnn…," Dark Peter winces in pain as one arm is rendered useless in the bear's great maw. "You… are… in… my… WAY!" Dark Peter bellows out as he takes the severed claw and slices across the bear's immense face.

"Arrrr….!" Dark Peter feels and hears his body being crunched by these huge jaws of death. He lifts up the claw once more and slashes into the enormous eye. The Bear God reels back in pain, dropping its prey to the ground. "Even a god can bleed!" Dark Peter recovers from his fall and prepares for the repercussions from taking out Artikos' right eye.

The bear charges in a mad rage, "Come on. Come on…," Dark Peter remains patient–still as a statue–as the enraged bear swallows him whole in one big gulp. Moments later a crimson streak envelops the white fur on the bear's neck. Its one eye rolls back into its eye as it slams to the ground–shaking the entire village–breaking a part of the landmass off into the arctic waters beyond.

The villagers scream as Dark Peter cuts his way out of the gigantic bear's throat, breathing the cold air once more, freed from the powerful jaws of death into the frozen air above.

"Damn!" Peter grabs his lower back to stretch out his frame. "Stupid bear," he surveys the dead bear and empty village. Then, he proceeds to cut himself a trophy and a snack from his kill.

Belsnickel

Chapter 5

Whipper of Children

The Sami people do not take kindly to the killing and desecration of their bear god, Artikos. Dark Peter is pelted with rocks and sticks from a distance while donning his new white fur coat and headgear with matching boots. He pays no mind to the locals' insults and shouts, as he munches on the heart and continues on his journey.

Unbeknownst to Dark Peter, several sets of eyes from the frozen forest watch him from afar. Hours more hiking bring him to a small village on the outskirts of Lapland. "Now where would I be if I were a child whipper?" Looking around the village thinking where his next hunt should be.

Dark Peter scours the village in search of his query with no avail. He hears the faint sobbing of a child and walks toward the crying to investigate. He stands before a small broken down house abandoned years before. Dark Peter climbs the wobbly steps and one swift kick topples the old door hanging on by one old, rusty hinge. "What do we have here?"

"Who are you to be barging in on my home, stranger?" Dark Peter sees the host of the faceless voice. A plump man in a disheveled suit, carrying a switch in each hand – caught in the act of whipping two children's backs. The children's backs are riddled with whelps and bruises.

"What? You don't recognize me, cousin?" Dark Peter takes a step forward.

Frau
Perchta

Chapter 6

Christmas Witch

"Don't let her catch you sleeping, brother. You'll wake up with your belly full of straw and pebbles. Ho, ho, ho!" Santa's broad belly jiggles jovially with his sarcasm.

"Hmmmph! Not funny. Any ideas of her whereabouts?" Dark Peter grows impatient.

"Last time that I heard anything about her, she was in the outskirts of Lapland. That's all I can tell you."

"I shall seek her out," Dark Peter prepares to begin his next quest.

"By the way, brother, where did you come by the new attire?"

Smiling at Nicholas, "I killed Artikos."

"What?" Nicholas looks stunned by the answer as Dark Peter disappears into the cold night.

Dark Peter can still feel many sets of eyes upon him as his journey continues on, he stops periodically, but nothing manifests, eventually ignoring and forgetting it. The journey takes him to the Alps. The Alpine festival is in full swing as the townspeople celebrate with a parade featuring folks dressed in bright, traditional costumes– Santa Claus, The Krampus, elves, and many more. Dark Peter laughs to himself as he spies a townsman dressed up as he once dressed nearly a millennium ago. "I can't believe that I…," he stops his sentence as he catches sight of something down an alleyway not far from the festival.

Upon inspection of the alleyway, Dark Peter discovers several bodies–some men, some women, some children, but all have the same patterns of mutilation. Their stomachs ripped wide open, their innards replaced with straw and rocks, and their bodies cold as the ice he was walking upon. "Damn," Dark Peter utters as he bends down to inspect the bodies further. "You have been busy, Bright One." Standing up, he surveys an endless trail of slit-bellies. Dark Peter follows the obvious path – leading him to his new quarry.

The trail of mutilated corpses comes to a halt after a zig-zag of turns through the many alley ways.

"Pagan!" A female voice screams from behind Dark Peter. "Die!" A tall, slender woman with pale skin and golden hair rushes toward Dark Peter, startling him as she spears him to the ground. Upon her golden mane of hair, three-foot antlers with tips as sharp as arrows. They rake and swipe across Dark Peter. "Die!"

"Perchta! Damn you! It's me!"

Hesitating for a moment, "Zwarte? Why are you here?"

Raising back to his feet and offering his hand out to his assailant, "My brother sent me to find you."

"Hmmmph! What could he possibly want? I haven't heard from either of you in a millennium."

"He had me on ice," looking up at the rooftops to notice the straggele watching his every move. "Send your hounds away Perchta…or I'll make boots out of them like I did the bear god."

Frau Perchta snaps her fingers once and the demonic werewolves scatter from sight. "What does he want with me?"

"Something's going on with him, some kind of doomsday end of the world shit. I told him I would help him. I am bound to him."

Nodding to Dark Peter, she says, "I'll go peacefully, Zwarte."

"Not like you had a choice in the matter, my dear," he says, smiling at her, "You could ask Belsnickle, but his head is now detached from his body."

Frau Pechta's eyes grow wide from Dark Peter's statement. "Let's take leave now, Zwarte." She looks around for her straggele demons, but they are nowhere to be seen.

"They're nearby. They never stray too far away from you, Percht."

Nodding, "This is true, but they have been behaving rather peculiarly as of late; quite concerning."

Paying no mind to her, "Let's be off," the pair trek off, leaving the town behind them. They travel without any incident and stop to rest for a moment. "I can feel eyes watching us, Zwarte."

"Aye. Something has been following me for days. Whoever or whatever it is has been keeping its distance." Dark Peter takes a swig of water and hands the flock to Perchta.

"Let us rest here for the night?" She touches Dark Peter's chest. "Lay with me once more, like we did when we were younger?" She looks up into his eyes.

Dark Peter gives him a quick smile, "It has been a while since I had the touch of a woman." He pulls her up to him; using the pelt of Artikos, he covers them up beneath the snow white pelt. As they share a bed for the night, the passion they haven't felt in nearly a thousand years until finally sleep takes hold of them both. The cold night demands upon them, but the thick pelt of Artikos keeps them safe and warm.

JACK
FROST

Killer Snowman

Chapter 7

Jack Frost and Friends

Perchta awakens in the morning before Dark Peter as he snores like a hibernating bear would. Her snow white hair matches the frozen ground, her beautiful, but pale complexion grows even more translucent as she clears her eyes to see something more horrifying than she could ever have imagined. Her straggele demon followers – her most loyal, devoted friends – beheaded and disemboweled strewn around. The snow no longer white while scattered with their red bodies and horned heads laying across the white snow beside their passion drenched bodies. How would she not have known what was happening? Entrails are strewn about the campsite, displayed like ornaments and wreaths. "No, Zwarte! Get up!" Perchta yells out in a mad, scared rage.

"What is it?" Dark Peter rolls over to the sight of Perchta's demons ripped to pieces. "Damn!" He looks around to look for the source of the destruction.

A blinding flash of light highlighting the snow momentarily blinds Dark Peter and Perchta. "Well, well, well. Look who we have here." A high-pitched male voice speaks to them.

Dark Peter squints his eyes, trying to regain his sight, "Who…?"

A child-like man with wings hovers near Dark Peter – pale white skin, ebony eyes, and translucent wings – then lands on the ground flawlessly. "We've been following you, Pete. What are you up to?" The fairy man rubs his chin.

"Jack? Jack Frost? What the hell are you doing?" Dark Peter towers above the small Jack.

"Arrgh!" Perchta rushes toward Jack in a rampage. "You killed them!" She strikes Jack and he loses his footing.

"Owwww! They were getting too close to us. Sorry, hahaha! We had to put them down!"

"We? Who is 'we'?" Dark Peter's eyes sharpen on Jack, curiously with rage.

Jack whistles, and as he does, a massive fist the size of a tree, strikes Perchta, sending her flying into the woods.

"Perchta!" Dark Peter turns in time to glimpse her crashing into the thick trees of the forest. "Don't worry about the witch, Pete. Your hands are about to be very full. Let me introduce you to my motley crew. He bows to Dark Peter as he says, "The big guy who took out your girlfriend is Yeti – Oh, he's a real beast, too." A hulking fifty-foot tall albino bigfoot bellows and beats its chest. "Oh. Seems he likes you, Pete."

"What is the meaning of this, Jack?" Dark Peter clenches his fists tightly and his nails slice at his palm.

"That rhymed, Pete. Say hello to my killer snowman, Pete!" Snapping his fingers, a monstrous snowman formed from the ice and snow itself rises from behind Dark Peter. Looking down at him as Dark Peter looks up to make eye contact with the frozen monster. "Last, but not least, this is Pog-Nip." Jack opens his hand to reveal a six-inch version of himself. "I found her ages ago – the last of her kind – a race that outdates our kind, Pete."

Pog-Nip flies toward Dark Peter. "This one bad, Jack! Breaked the big bear in half, he did." Warning Jack in her high pitched tinkling voice sounding awfully like a bell.

"He did. Did he?" Jack sneers at Dark Peter. "Go to hell, Pete!" Jack uses his staff to emit a cold discharge of pure ice which envelops Dark Peter. "Back to the ice box for you!" Jack claps in his own acclamation.

Nearby, Perchta is being pummeled by the monstrous Yetti and the killer snowman, her once-beautiful face and antlers protruding from her head, now broken and shattered. Her face was swollen and bloody–unrecognizable. Jack and Pog-nip rush to join the silent, but deadly duo. "Kill the witch! Killed her goblin friends! Now kill her!" Pog-nip flies around watching the onslaught.

"Sorry, Perchta! Nothing personal...," pointing his staff at her. "We were sent to subdue Pete. You are just excess baggage."

Spitting blood, "Why Jack?" Perchta grabs onto Jack's leg, looking up at him from the ground.

Jack winks at the killer snowman as he delivers the killing blow, piercing Perchta's heart with a precision ice blade. Perchta's head falls lifelessly next to Jack's feet.

"Ding dong! Snowman kills the witch!" Pog-nip exclaims in her annoying chiming voice.

"Shut up, Pog-nip!" Jack looks at her annoyed.

From behind the quartet of bounty hunters and killers, a whistling sound grabs their attention just as an ice-covered boulder sails by Jack's head and slams into the gargantuan Yeti, causing it to crash into a dozen large pines. The pines shred like paper.

"Forget about me, Jack?" Dark Peter grabs Jack by the neck and squeezes. "Why did you attack us? Where's Perchta?"

"Dirt nap. Witch is taking. Long time, too." Pog-nip flies right at Dark Peter who in turn smacks at the three and a half inch action figure like a fairy, flicking her away with his pinky. "Owwww!"

"Now, Jack, answer my questions," he clenched tighter around Jack's throat.

"Accch....bounty...on your head, Pete...to bring you in alive." Jack gasps for air and attempts to kick out at Peter.

"Who?" Dark Peter senses the ground beneath him starting to rumble from being him. Just as the killer snowman manifests itself. Dark Peter hurls Jack around, smashing him directly into the towering icy frame of the bulky snowman. The frozen figure is shattered into countless tiny pieces of ice and snow immediately.

"Aaaaaa-aaay!" Jack screams in pain as he becomes embedded with icy shards. Dark Peter tightens his grip even more.

"Tell me, Jack. Last chance."

"Sorry, Pete. No…can…do." Jack continues to fight for air.

"Have it your way then." Dark Peter shrugs and squeezes Jack's neck as his head implodes. Dark Peter doesn't even flinch when he is splattered with blood.

"Holy! Jack's head went splat, splat, splat!" Pog-nip looks on in sheer horror.

"Go away!" Dark Peter shoos Pog-nip. He walks to his fallen companion, Perchta and pulls her up to him. Causing him to see the Yeti still unconscious from the boulder crashing into him.

"Sleeping, it is! From rock to the head. Mad it be when it wakes up," Pog-nip points and yells.

"Not for long," Dark Peter turns to the monstrous abominable snowman and in one swift twist with his massive arms, Dark Peter breaks the giant's neck while it slumbers.

"Kill it in its sleep, you did."

"It was your idea," Dark Peter shrugs and ventures back to Perchta's body. "Damn."

"Witch is dead. Jack is dead. Frosty gone. Squatch dead. Pog-nip is all alone again." Pog-nip sighs as Dark Peter buries Perchta's corpse under a blanket of snow. "Not going back to the creature to tell what happened to Jack. Creature will have to find out on its own, it will."

"What?" Dark Peter grabs the tiny humanoid insect, interrupting it. "Creature? That Jack's boss? Who?"

"Ugly creature! Stinking of death, it does," Pog-nip continues.

"Krampus," the name rolls off of Dark Peter's lips, "Where is he?"

"I can show you! Can take you to its den of death and stink."

Dark Peter releases her. "Don't make me regret this, Pog-nip."

THE KRAMPUS

Chapter 8

The Krampus

The Krampus – a thing of nightmares and death. German folklore describes him as a half-goat, half-demon – with a long tongue and horns, a thick dark fur coat and grotesque fangs.

The Krampus sits alone at a small fire in its dark, decaying cave – once home to a proud bear that fled after the Krampus's arrival.

"Who's there?" The Krampus sniffs the air. "Reveal yourself or your suffering will be legendary."

"Krampus," a voice calls out from the immense shadows.

"Who knows me by that name? Friend…or foe?"

"Surely you can recognize my voice? Or has it been that long?" Dark Peter steps into the light by the fire.

"Zwarte Piet?" Sitting back down by the fire. "What brings you here to the Tyrolean Mountains? Did you bring any naughty children?" Spying Pog-nip with Dark Peter. "Or perhaps a naughty fairy?" The Krampus snickers and smirks.

"No," Dark Peter sits down across from the Krampus, maintaining eye contact the whole time. "I'm going to ask–once and only once–Krampus, did you put a bounty on my head for Jack Frost to collect?" Standing up, slowly as he stares down the Krampus.

The beastly Krampus stands up growling, showing its teeth. "No. Hahaha!"

Turning from a laugh to a stone cold look. "If I had wanted you, I would have hunted you down myself, Zwarte. I would have split you from gullet to groin with my claws. You are not unattainable."

"Pog-nip! Is this the creature which Jack met with? Tell me!"

"Ugly! Ugly! Yes, yes. But smells different! Not same one!" Pog-nip answers decisively.

"I told you, Zwarte Piet. I do not lie. Join me for Krampusnacht." He extends his clawed hand. "This will be my forgiveness for your accusations."

"No, I have other matters to attend to. We will take our leave now."

"You're not leaving here alive, Zwarte. Join me or join my fire spit."

Dark Peter grins slightly, "So be it." The two engage in close combat. The Krampus was much larger and broader than Dark Peter, but just as strong. He holds his own. "Your breath smells of shit, Krampus."

"Soon it shall smell like your cooked flesh, Zwarte!" The Krampus swipes at Dark Peter with its massive claws shredding open his chest, causing deep wounds that bleed profusely.

"Aaaaa!" Dark Peter howls in pain grabbing at his wounds, trying to stamp out the blood.

"Tasting his claws, "Your blood is so sweet, Zwarte. I am going to devour you raw." In a frenzied rage, Krampus rushes toward the injured Dark Peter. It roars as it sprints to land, killing blow to Dark Peter, a blast of pure ice strikes the Krampus in its eyes, briefly stunning him.

"Aaaaa! What sorcery is this?" Placing his giant claw hands to his blinded eyes.

"Now! Now Dark one! Stake the stinky creature!" Pog-nip shouts to Dark Peter immediately after she ice sprays the Krampus's eyes with her awe-inspiring eldritch cold blast.

Without hesitation, Dark Peter, writhing in pain, manages to secure the spit spindle from the fire and rams it deep into Krampus's chest cavity of the monstrous beast. "Die! Damn you!" Dark Peter presses the hot metal deeper into his chest void of a feeling heart. It slumps and looks up at Dark Peter.

"He … will … betray … you … again …, Zwarte," with his final words, the Krampus drops to the ground – dead. Black blood, the same consistency of bile, oozes from the gaping chasm that Dark Peter created in his chest.

Dark Peter spits down on the Krampus. "Your advice falls upon deaf ears, fool."

"Kill him good, you did," Pog-nip chips in rather excitedly.

"I didn't need any help," Dark Peter swats Pog-nip to the ground. He sits down by the fire and tends to his wounds.

"Owwww! Pog-nip save you, dark one!"

"Shut up. How did Frost put up with you? And why?"

Pog-nip flies to Dark Peter's shoulder, "Pog-nip useful! Dark one see, he will."

"We shall see," Dark Peter snaps one of the Krampus's legs off from the hip bone and places it upon the fire spit. The coarse hair burns quickly as a torrid stench worse than anything fills the cave and air alike.

"Yuck! Stinky creature stinks even more when cooked," Pog-nip is repulsed by the aroma.

"Ever had a goat by a campfire?" Dark Peter laughs with his full belly as Pog-nip wretches and vomits more than one could imagine from a being so tiny. "Ha! Ha! Ha!"

Rangifer
Tarandus

Chapter 9

Reindeer Games

Morning arises. The fire in the Krampus's cave has died into cold soot and ashes; a giant leg bones lay on the ground nearby – bare of any meat or sinew.

"Ate the Krampus, we did," Pog-nip voice chimes from her sleep, which awakens Dark Peter, his wounds still paining him.

"She never shuts up," Dark Peter mutters to the fallen Krampus as he stands and stretches. He walks out from the cave to begin his day's tasks, relieving himself, and taking to his journey. "Pog-nip, awaken now. We take our leave from this vile place."

The pair set off on the white tundra terrain. Dark Peter looks at the sun's position to determine his directions.

"How did you end up with Frost?" Dark Peter asks.

"Asleep, I was. But…Jack found me and took the tiny one in, he did. Cruel he was to Pog-nip. Good riddance!" Pog-nip answers.

"Stop!" Dark Peter states firmly, startling Pog-nip. "You feel that?" Dark Peter is frozen in his tracks as the earth beneath him begins to tremor and shake.

"Big! Real big!" Pog-nip points to the horizon as golden antlers reflect against the sun's light causing Pog-nip and Dark Peter to be blinded briefly. What enters the plateau stands on all four of its deeply cloven hooves. Each one the size of a wagon wheel. Twenty-feet tall and excess of a ton.

White fur and antlers fifteen feet tall and sharp as knives.

"What… the hell… is THAT?" Dark Peter stares at the giant reindeer as it snorts, pawing the ground in an act of aggression, so primal and animalistic.

"Rangifer Tarandus, it is. Legendary. So mean! Mean!" Pog-nip stares in awe at the beast before them.

"Hmmmph! Guess that's why this land is uninhabitable."

"Run! Run! Flee, Darkest one." Pog-nip screams in fear.

Throwing off the polar bear god's pelt-fashioned cloak. "Just to be trampled underneath it? I think not." He expands his form and stands his ground.

The gigantic reindeer lowers its head and charges at Dark Peter.

"Ummmm!" Dark Peter clenches his abs, bracing himself as he grabs hold of the wide, enormous antlers. If not for Dark Peter's herculean strength, he would have been stomped underfoot, but his smaller size cannot stop the beast from flipping him into the air like a mere children's toy.

"Dammit!" Dark Peter knows he's in a vulnerable state. Pog-nip can only watch in horror as the monster takes its head and shakes Dark Peter around with its bony antlers, cutting and piercing him continuously...eventually impaling him. Flinging him to the side, he loses interest. The monstrous reindeer leaves the battlefield – no longer feeling threatened over its territory.

"Dark one! Dark one! You are live?" Pog-nip flies to Dark Peter in haste.

Dark Peter groans as his eyes roll back into his head and his hands clench at his exposed intestines. The gaping hole in his side, seeping blood across the snowy ground below him. Looking at Pog-nip, "Get... Help...," Dark Peter passes out, imploring his only ally.

"Dark one! Dark one! Dark one...," Pog-nip keeps shouting at Dark Peter. The light in his eyes fades to black. He is reminded of the feeling of freezing into nothingness in his brother's darkened basement at his brother's cabin.

Hans Trapp

Chapter 10

Hans Trapp

"Dark one! Dark one! Wakey, wakey."
Pog-nip buzzes around Dark Peter's head in
an attempt to beckon him awake.

"Where? Where am I?" Dark Peter
slowly opens his eyes, his vision quite foggy.
A figure begins to manifest in front of him. A
figure dressed as a scarecrow.

"Hans…von…Trotha," Dark Peter
whispers, still groggy.

"Your companion found me and brought me to you, Zwarte. Nasty wound, but I mended you the best that I could," he leans down to look into Dark Peter's face.

"You reek of death and shit, Hans." Dark Peter turns his head away from the frightening scarecrow figure.

"Do not fear me, Zwarte. I am not going to eat you." Looking to Pog-nip, "But I may roast your tiny companion.

Pog-nip gulps as she can feel the sinister eyes preying upon her.

"I am ashamed, my savior in arms was a butcher and eater of children," Dark Peter speaks, facing away from the Trapp.

"How dare you judge me, Zwarte?" He points directly at Dark Peter. "Have you forgotten your banishment? He sent you to the northern hemisphere. El Pedro Negro! Stealing children in the dead of the night."

Sitting up, stiffly, "Ummm," in pain still. "We are nothing alike, butcher. I was doing what I was told unlike you… you lost his favor ages ago."

"That's all you ever cared for. His favor! His blessings. But you are right, you do do as you are told… and I get to do as I please."

"Your greed consumed you, you sold your soul to the devil," Dark Peter continues the argument.

"Ah! The same devil who bestowed me with the power to save you, Zwarte! If you survive the night, you shall become my thrall – my champion when the final battle begins."

Dark Peter rises to his feet, "I'll never serve you…, butcher!" He steadies himself, preparing for battle.

"You are in no shape to fight me, Zwarte."

Dark Peter grabs hold of the skinny scarecrow, "And you're in no shape, but straw!" He pulls apart the butcher of children – pieces of burlap and straw fall to the ground and fly about the room. Not even a scream or a sound emerges from Hans Trapp as Dark Peter rips him apart. He falls to the ground. He is still weak from his encounter with the giant Rangifer.

"Dark one! Dark one! You okay?" Pog-nip quickly buzzes to his side to survey him.

"Just weak…tired."

"Scarecrow man, creepy! Good riddance."

"If you only knew, Pog-nip! Keep watch over me while I rest for what is to come."

"What coming, Dark one?" She looks at Dark Peter in confusion.

"Hans Trapp made a deal with the devil. He will be here tonight to claim my soul. I must be ready," Dark Peter closes his eyes.

Pog-nip watches the horizon constantly for any movement as the dark hours click on throughout the night.

Mari
Lwyd.

Chapter 11

Mari Lwyd Comes A Knocking

Pog-nip is startled by a loud knock upon the door. She peeks through a window to see a white horse skull creature licking at the door with its elongated tongue. It is a thing of nightmares – a zombie horse sent from the other side to carry Zwarte off to hell. There are no eyeballs in the hollow sockets, but still knowing Pog-nip is there, it turns to see her as she freezes in mid-air, paralyzed in pure terror.

The zombie nightmare begins kicking away at the door, senses its quarry inside…incapacitated. With one more hard, swift kick to the door, it opens. Mari Lwyd enters, seeming to chant or sing a song before it makes off with the unforgiven, forsaken soul it seeks.

It nudges closer and closer to the sleeping Dark Peter to claim him. The zombie horse monster's jaw goes ajar as a freezing blast of cold ice sprays the undead beast in the face.

"Back off, horse skully! Dark one not be taken this night." Pog-nip's fear is overridden by her loyalty. She feverishly attacks the skeleton underworld horse. She continues her barrage of ice spells, Mari Lwyd slowly backs away from the relentless assault from the tiny combatant. "Dark One! Wakey. Please!"

At that precise moment, Dark Peter opens his eyes and hurls his body as a projectile into the framework of bones – the zombie horse is splintered into pieces, cascading in every direction.

Dark Peter roars like a lion in victorious pride, "Come Pog-nip. We're leaving this vile place."

"Where go we, Dark One?" Pog-nip lands upon his shoulder, exhausted from her onslaught on the zombie horse. Dark Peter carrying a zombie skull in his sack as a prize.

Chapter 12

Santa's Confession

"Don't just sit there with that glum look on your face, brother. Are you going to quit playing these Go Fetch games with me and tell me what the hell is going on here?" Dark Peter confronts his brother, Saint Nicholas.

Santa Claus thinks momentarily before answering, "I don't know what game you're referring to, brother. You're helping me… us," he makes eye contact with Pog-nip, "My… my… where did you find your little companion?"

"She was with Frost when he tried to kill me … killing Perchta instead." Dark Peter growls deep in his chest.

Pog-nip stares at Saint Nicholas before darting back to Dark Peter's shoulder and begins to whisper. "Fat Krampus he is. Talk, talk to Jack. Clothed in Krampus cloth he was."

"What??" Dark Peter looks at Pog-nip in disbelief. Putting his hand around Santa's throat…, "Were you masquerading around as the Krampus? Conspiring with Jack Frost? To kill me and Perchta?" He is screaming at him, uncontrollably.

Gasping for air, Santa pleads, "N…no. Not kill you, just…just…keep…an eye…on you…your progress," his face turns beet red then purples.

Loosening his grip, "Progress on what?"

"The mission, Peter. Perchta's demons got too close. Jack was never to engage you. Her death was never to happen."

Dark Peter slams his fist into the wall, creating a hole and making the walls shake.

"Secret missions… Perchta's death… Your bounty hunters following me… a giant fucking reindeer. Hans Trapp saved me only to use me as a herald. Mari Lwyd coming for my soul. What else is there, brother?"

Sighing, "Damnit, Jack Frost!" Santa growls in frustration.

"He's dead now. I crushed his skull."

"Another potential ally for…," he pauses rather than finish his sentence.

"Who? Who is it that you fear?" Dark Peter watches his brother closely, awaiting an honest answer.

Sighing, "Alas, I must tell you … what is about to manifest in these dark days ahead."

Dark Peter crosses his arms, "Go on."

"Lussi has been incensed with a maddening rage. She is coming and hell's coming with her."

"The angel? Lussi?" Questioning Saint Nicholas.

"Yes, she has fallen from grace and is now intent on total destruction and devastation. There will be nothing left." He lowers his head.

"Angel bad. Bad! Bad!" Pog-nip panics and flies about the room.

"Then why send me on these wild hunts? This makes no sense!"

"Ahhhh, but it does, Peter. For every evil you have snuffed out, the less to join her army out of fear."

"Can we reason with her? Surely she has some sort of sense left?" Dark Peter asks.

"I have tried," shaking his head, "she seeks the sword of heaven… to end us all."

"I'm done with this," Dark Peter states.

Saint Nicholas takes a deep breath, "Don't you walk away from me! You're in this, too!" Raising his voice to Dark Peter.

"Come, Pog-nip!" Dark Peter motions for her to follow him.

"She will be coming for you, too, Peter/ You will either join her or die by her hand. Possibly, even both."

Dark Peter spits at Santa's feet, "I'm not your whipping boy anymore."

"Do this, brother… I'll redeem you… for everything… even your time in the south."

"No more ice boxes? Tricks or banishments, either, brother? I'll do this – not for you, but for me. Just me."

Whispering under his breath, "Thank God."

"Where, brother?" Dark Peter snarls.

"Gryla. Find Gryla and her children. Lussi won't be far behind."

"And you, brother? Where are you going to be? Hiding? Cowering away while I do your dirty work?" Grinning at Santa with a mad gleam in his eye.

"I will be here planning for if you fall."

"You and I will settle up, brother; when I return." Dark Peter and Pog-nip leave with haste from Saint Nicholas's quarters.

"I pray the two of you slay each other, brother," Santa says as he returns to his chair in comfort.

Chapter 13

Gryla

Dark Peter and Pog-nip watch from the top of the highwall, paying attention to the Ogre. The ogre, Gryla, is there directing her twisted half-human, half-ogre children as they enter the mine, acting as ants, carrying rock and debris out from inside of the mountain walls. Keeping an eye out for the yule cat as well. Since it is nowhere to be seen. The children were chanting a poem in menacing voices, "You all know the Yule…

huge indeed…." They move about in weird manners, doing their tasks.

"...didn't know where he came from… or where he went…," Pog-nip joins their song. Pog-nip sniffs the air, "Phew… stinky smell. What smells? Horrible! Horrible!"

Dark Peter inhales the aroma, "Gryla's stewpot – full of scared children – who shit themselves."

Pog-nip watches the ogre giantess stir her pot of severed arms, heads, legs, and other various body parts. Mixing about her large cauldron. One of her maladjusted children, known as Potscraper, gets a scolding from Gryla for trying to snatch a child's leg from the boiling pot.

A couple of his brothers come over to join in the beating of the thief, only to have Gryla stop them abruptly and look straight up the mountain ledge that holds Dark Peter and Pog-nip. She points and the three Yule lads – deformed and depraved – sprint up the mountainside as fast as they possibly can.

"She heard us whispering in the wind. Our element of surprise is now gone." Dark Peter undoes his cloak of polar bear god, dropping it to the ground to prepare for battle.

"Ugly! Ugly! Ugly!" Pog-nip yells out as the Yule lads get closer and closer, each one more gross and perverted than the one before.

"He opened his glaring… eyes…," they sing as they climb closer. "The two of them are glowing bright…" The three approaching are Gluggagaegir – also known as Window Peeper, Ketrokur – also known as Meat-Hook, and Pot Scraper. Short legs, stubbly bodies, elongated arms, and large heads. All with the same angry faces.

They were right upon the much taller Dark Peter who grabs hold of Window Peeper by the neck, hoisting him high into the air. "Run, run back to mommy," he squeezes the Yule lad's neck, severing it from the half-ogre body. The beheaded corpse flops onto the icy ground, spewing blood onto the white surface. "Go or suffer the same fate."

The two Yule lads look at each other, then turn and bound back down the same hill that they climbed just minutes before. An overcast shadow moves over Dark Peter.

"Dark one?" Pog-nip tries to get Dark Peter's attention.

Dark Peter turns around, "Shit."

The sight before him, humbles him to his core as Jolakotturinn – the Yule Cat – a huge and vicious cat, that had been lurking about the frosty countryside heard the commotion and came to investigate.

Pog-nip stares up at him, "It took a really brave man…to look him in the eyes…," her song continues.

Yule
Cat

Chapter 14

Yule Cat

The terrifying cat hisses and its glossy black fur stands on end as it stares down at him… it begins to circle its prey. His whiskers were sharp as bristles while his massive paws with arched claws sharp upon the snow.

"I'm so sick of giant fucking animals," Dark Peter sighs.

"A terrible sight… he gave a wave of his strong tail…," the children at the base of the hill still sing.

The cat jumps about clawing the ground and hissing, "...he roamed at large, hungry and evil...So so evil." Pog-nip continued to sing her chiming, bell voice.

The Yule Cat emits a low, rumbling growl before it pounces onto Dark Peter sinking its teeth into his shoulder. "Aaarrrgh!" He reels in agony from the vicious bite. "Get... off... me!" Dark Peter grabs at the monster cat by its massive black furry head and flips it over his body. It lands gracefully on all four feet, unscathed and ready for another strike.

In the background, all the while, he hears the children, "People shudder at his name... hear 'meow'... evil will happen soon...".

"Dark One! Dark One! Bad kitty. Dark one bleed all round. He no like mice only men," Pog-nip panics and zips around the battlefield, but continues the song until she sees who is coming. "Ogre come now, she is."

Gryla is approaching with several more of her grotesque children, unknownst if they are to join the frey or watch the battle ensue. The children are still chanting the song, "Mustn't let him get the children… they had to get something new to wear… for all who did… were free of that cat's grasp."

In a rough, raspy voice, Gryla speaks, "Kill him! Add him to the pot."

Without hesitation, her loyal pet, the Yule Cat lunges for Dark Peter once more, but this time, he is more prepared and catches the cat by the open jaws. Just mere inches from Dark Peter's face. The hot stench of death permeates from his nostrils. "Ummmm!" Dark Peter can feel his leverage loosen as the monster cat begins to overpower him. Quickly thinking, Dark Peter drops to his knees, using the cat's momentum to sail through the air and down the icy slope, giving pause to its engagement with Dark Peter.

"Goody good good!" Pog-nip claps in joy.

"Shut up, Pog-nip!" Dark Peter looks at her annoyed, "It will be back and angrier still."

"Nothing angrier than Dark One!" Pog-nip replies.

Dark Peter turns his attention to the giant ogress as she approaches. "Leave this place, Gryla. Take your children with you… while you still can." Flexing in an attempt to intimidate the freakish ogress, eater of children.

Not backing down, "You are the one who shall leave, Zwarte. Walk away or become shit as we pass your innards through our gullets." The Yule lads who had accompanied their mother laugh and snicker as she mocks Dark Peter.

"Whether he still exists…I not know…," Pog-nip sings beside the children.

"But his visit would be in vain, if next time everybody got something new to wear…you may be thinking helping…where help is needed," the children cackle as they work to sing their song, "Perhaps searching for those who live in a lightless world will give a happy day…" They look at Pog-nip and giggle.

"And a merry, merry Yule," Pog-nip answers their wanton looks with the finishing of their song in her chiming voice.

"I think not!" Dark Peter ignores the children and swings a haymaker punch at the taller Gryla, barely flinching, spitting out a tooth after the strike from Dark Peter. "Shit."

Gryla grins as the Yule Cat has returned, towering behind its owner, hissing – eyes locked onto Dark Peter.

A thunderous boom from the mountainside distracts everyone from Dark Peter, Gryla, the Yule Cat, Pog-nip, and the Yule Lads alike. The lads mutter amongst themselves, "They are closer to finding it," Gryla exclaims, "Shoo! Shoo! Go to help your brothers." She orders them back to the cavern and mountainside. They quickly scurry forth. Gryla pats her cat upon the head, "Now, eat him," she turns and follows after her many children.

Dark Peter measures the cat once more, knowing the beast is relentless and aggressive. "I swear I am going to kill you, Cat. I will wear your fur." The cat swipes at Dark Peter with its razor sharp six-inch claws.

"You did it, Dark one!" Pog-nip becomes overjoyed.

"Shut up! What in the hell are you talking about?" Dark Peter never removes his eyes from the over-large cat.

"Have new clothes, you do. Legend song. Cat no eat new clothes," Pog-nip cheers excitedly near him.

Dark Peter's eyes open wide, "Damnit! She's right," he mumbles to himself. Then he tumbles and rolls to where he disrobed from his polar bear cloak earlier when his battle had ensued.

Dark Peter holds the thick, massive white cloak up to the gigantic cat. Its blazing red eyes lock onto the garment as he sniffs deeply at it.

"Is working. Dark One." Pog-nip's patience is spent.

"I don't know! Legends aren't always accurate," Dark Peter scolds Pog-nip.

The monstrous cat begins to purr then rub its head on Dark Peter as if pleased with the new attire.

"Worked, it did!" Pog-nip cheers excitedly.

Dark Peter pets the Yule Cat, "Good work, Pog-nip, but we're not quite done yet. Down the hillside!"

Pog-nip nods and follows him.

Lussi

Chapter 15

Lussi

Still reeling and aching from the battle with the monstrous Yule Cat, Dark Peter takes deep breaths as he reaches the bottom of the icy, snowy hillside. He looks back to see the gigantic black cat, still standing upon the hill.

Another thunderous boom shakes and rumbles through the foundation of the frozen plateau. The heavens, themselves, open up from the sky, clouds part wide, and bright rays of light shine down onto the snowy ground, blinding everyone and everything in the vicinity.

"Fuck," Dark Peter utters as the sight begins to return and the sight before him is both beautiful and horrifying.

A beautiful woman in a white robe and sash descends upon the mountainside. Her elliptical wings spread out dilly as she lands gracefully upon the ground. A crown of lit candles rests upon her blonde-flowing hair. She makes eye contact with Dark Peter with her empty, black eye sockets and droplets of blood oozing from their voids – two open orifices that once held her glowing jade green eyes.

"Shit!" Pog-nip says, frozen in fear. Dark Peter looks at her.

Gryla and two of the three Yule lads approach Lussi. "We welcome you, Lussi. Our master," Gryla kneels before the angel and the Yule lads follow suit with their mother.

Lussi backhands Gryla, knocking her to the giant ogress backwards, "Your usefulness has worn its welcome out, hideous one." Lussi speaks in a demonic voice. She picks up the Yule lad Stufur – also known as Stubby, opening her maw and biting his head clean off. His body twitches and then goes limp. "Bring me my sword before I bite all of your heads off, lads."

Quaking with fear, the lads that were inside the mining cave appear, three of them carrying an ominous silver and gold long sword, dragging it by the hilt. Fire dances along the blade, leaving a burnt trail behind it as it is dragged.

"Hurry up, grotesque ones. So I may gut you and end your filthy existence!" Lussi bellows orders loudly to the lads.

"Fire sword… bad… bad! End of times!" Pog-nip begins yapping erratically.

Dark Peter whispers, "Not today! Not by HER!" He steps between the Yule Lads and Lussi, preventing her from acquiring the sword from them.

"Who dares?" Lussi boils over with anger, staring down Dark Peter, "Step aside."

"No," Dark Peter stands firm in his defiance, "I don't know you, but I do know Saint Lucia."

"I am no longer a saint," she gives a sinister grin to Dark Peter, "Who are you, dark one? Tell me before I flay you and use your skin as my new sheath for my shiny new sword."

"I have many names – Zwarte Piet, El Pedro Negro, Dark Peter... and many more. Your plans are those of madness."

"Mad? I sense your anger and rage, dark one. It excites me, it almost matches my own fury." The candles upon her crown flicker with excitement. "Join me... or join my army of demons... as fodder and food." She points to the sky, showing Dark Peter an endless army of flying ghouls and devils.

"The sword shall not be wielded by you, Lussi." Dark Peter clenches his fists tightly.

"I know you not, not now, nor after I slay you and desecrate your carcass." Lussi lunges for Dark Peter. He grabs hold of her, trying to keep her away from the sword.

"You're strong and angry dark one! I have slain countless like you, turned cities into salt I have fought in heaven and hell. What do you say, dark one?" Lussi overpowers Dark Peter, slinging him aside. She inches closer to her prize, the sword of the heavens. "Hidden from me for centuries ever since the first war in heaven. Now, heaven and hell shall be one and the same." She reaches for the sword, drawn to it. The Yule lads drop the hilt and scatter like cockroaches.

"Arrrrrr!" Dark Peter roars like a lion and tackles Lussi, mounting her and pinning her down. He begins to pummel her with his massive rock-like hands – way-laying into her face. "Grrrr!" Dark Peter growls like a wild animal as he assaults her.

"Hahahaha!" Lussi laughs at Dark Peter and his best efforts. Her candles flame higher, burning brighter than ever. "Yes! Your rage fuels me!" She reaches up, seizing Dark Peter by the throat.

"Unch…," Dark Peter has never felt any strangle hold like this one. He grabs her arm, trying to break the death grip she has on him.

"Where's that rage now? All I sense is fear," Lussi begins to rise up just as Pog-nip rushes in to attack Lussi with a cold base attack from her fingertips.

"Let go! Go! Go!" Pog-nip screams at Lussi as ice as cold as the arctic pelts Lussi's angelic-demonic face.

Begone, gnat!" Lussi swats at Pog-nip, missing her, but the air behind the swing sends her sailing into a snowbank, burying her away.

Dark Peter regains his balance and back to his feet, holding his neck with one hand.

"This game is over," Lussi ignores Peter and turns once more to the sword. "Finally," she reaches for the prize.

Before she can even touch the hilt of the blazing sword, a huge black shadow of fangs and fur pounces down upon the fallen angel's back, biting and tearing at her.

"What manner of beast is this?" Lussi speaks out as the Yule Cat continues its attack on the angel. She shrugs off the onslaught, even as the cat rips her robe and body alike. Blood flies about like rainfall, but Lussi never falters. She backhands the monster cat … it staggers and falls from the impact.

At that very instant, Dark Peter acts and grabs hold of Lussi's left wing. He pulls and turns it with all of his strength, he can muster. He begins to feel it tearing away from her back.

"Aieee!" Lussi screams.

Dark Peter uses her pain as a tool and wrenches the wing even more, twisting it, and in one mighty pull, he rips her wing off of her. "Aieeee!" Lussi drops to her knees in pain. "Dark… one. I am going to kill you slowly for this outrage."

"Shut up!" Dark Peter in one motion picks up the flaming sword of the heavens and swings it down upon Lussi's candle crowned head. The crown splits along with her head in two, breaking the sword upon impact.

Lussi opens her mouth in an attempt to speak, but all that expels is black blood. Her candle crown extinguished – falls down into the snow – smoldering.

The Yule Cat awake now growls and begins to feast upon the now twice-fallen angel.

Dark Peter surveys the battlefield, finding and extracting the unconscious Pog-nip from the snow and places her into his hands. His first sign of tenderness.

Chapter 16

Revelations

Entering the decorated shack, adorned in wreaths, garlands, and warmth, "It is all done now, brother." Dark Peter looks Santa Claus in the eyes. "Just as you asked. It is done."

"Ho! Ho! Ho!" Santa Claus rejoices. "I had no doubt, Zwarte. I knew you would succeed. What of the sword?"

"Destroyed along with Lussi."

"Hmmmph, well, good," Santa seems off as he runs his hand through his white beard.

"The Yule Cat and remaining Yule lads have sworn fealty to me as well." Dark Peter continues.

"Hmmph…odd, but nonetheless. Come sit with me, by my side, brother. You deserve it." Santa opens his arms to Dark Peter and the two embrace.

Dark Peter whispers something to Santa, as Santa's smile turns to sadness. Santa looks down to see his hands being taken by the Yule lads. "What is this, brother?" He looks up to see that Dark Peter has a shard of the sword of the heavens.

It slices into his arms, removing his hands. "You are done delivering presents to ungrateful children," he declares and Santa faints from the pain. Santa's hat falls into the pool of his own blood. "Remove his body from my sight. He can heal with his minions in my usual room," Dark Peter ascends to his brother's chair, picking up the blood-soaked hat and placing it upon his head.

Pog-nip reluctantly speaks to Dark Peter, "What wish you, Dark one? You charge now."

Smiling, "Ready the Yule Cat and Lads, we're going giant reindeer hunting," he stares at Pog-nip.

All alone, Dark Peter looks at the blood on the wooden floor of his fallen brother, "Hahaha! Ha ho ha ho! Ho, ho, ho!" As he turns to follow his crew out, his finger goes up and taps the bridge of his nose.

Dark Peter

The End!

The Yule Cat

By Johannes ur Kottlum

You all know the Yule Cat
And that Cat was huge indeed.
People didn't know where he came from
Or where he went.
He opened his glaring eyes wide,
The two of them glowing bright.
It took a really brave man
To look straight into them.
His whiskers, sharp as bristles,
His back arched up high.
And the claws of his hairy paws
Were a terrible sight.
He gave a wave of his strong tail,
He jumped and he clawed and he hissed.
Sometimes up in the valley,

Sometimes down by the shore.

He roamed at large, hungry and evil

In the freezing Yule snow.

In every home

People shuddered at his name.

If one heard a pitiful "meow"

Something evil would happen soon.

Everybody knew he hunted men

But didn't care for mice.

He picked on the very poor

That no new garments got

For Yule – who toiled

And lived in dire need.

From them he took in one fell swoop

Their whole Yule dinner

Always eating it himself

If he possibly could.

Hence it was that the women

At their spinning wheels sat

Spinning a colorful thread

For a frock or a little sock.

Because you mustn't let the Cat

Get hold of the little children.

They had to get something new to wear

From the grownups each year.

And when the lights came on, on Yule Eve

And the Cat peered in,

The little children stood rosy and proud

All dressed up in their new clothes.

Some had gotten an apron

And some had gotten shoes

Or something that was needed

– That was all it took.

For all who got something new to wear

Stayed out of that pussy-cat's grasp

He then gave an awful hiss

But went on his way.

Whether he still exists I do not know.

But his visit would be in vain

If next time everybody

Got something new to wear.

Now you might be thinking of helping

Where help is needed most.

Perhaps you'll find some children

That have nothing at all.

Perhaps searching for those

That live in a lightless world

Will give you a happy day

And a Merry, Merry Yule.

MORE WORKS BY THE AUTHOR

Trepidation Volumes 1-4, Bloody Mercy, Glass Trepidation, Fairy Tales of Trepidation, 150 Jokes of Trepidation, and Mangled Dolls of Trepidation.
Available on Amazon.com.

Coming Soon

Ever wonder about the Urban Legends around you? The ones that go bump in the night beside you as you try to sleep? Keep an eye out for the riveting breakdown of what they just might be.